Please visit our web site at: **www.garethstevens.com**
For a free color catalog describing Gareth Stevens Publishing's list of high-quality books and multimedia programs, call 1-800-542-2595 (USA) or 1-800-387-3178 (Canada). Gareth Stevens Publishing's fax: (414) 332-3567.

Library of Congress Cataloging-in-Publication Data

Ridinger, Gayle.
    [Stella in fondo al mare. English]
    A star at the bottom of the sea / written by Gayle Ridinger; illustrated by Andreina Parpajola.
      p. cm.
    Summary: With help from her undersea friends, a starfish travels to the sky where she wants to shine and dance like the other stars, but she quickly discovers that things are not always as they appear.
    ISBN 0-8368-3175-6 (lib. bdg.)
    [1. Starfish—Fiction. 2. Stars—Fiction. 3. Constellations—Fiction. 4. Marine animals—Fiction.]
    I. Parpajola, Andreina, ill. II. Title.
PZ7.R4255St 2002
[Fic]—dc21
                                  2002017673

This North American edition first published in 2002 by
Gareth Stevens Publishing
A World Almanac Education Group Company
330 West Olive Street, Suite 100
Milwaukee, WI 53212 USA

Gareth Stevens editor: Dorothy L. Gibbs
Cover design: Tammy Gruenewald

This edition © 2002 by Gareth Stevens, Inc. Original edition published as *Una stella in fondo al mare* © 2001 by Edizioni Arka, Milano, Italy.

Printed in the United States of America

1 2 3 4 5 6 7 8 9 06 05 04 03 02

A Star at the Bottom of the Sea

Written by Gayle Ridinger
Illustrations by Andreina Parpajola

Gareth Stevens Publishing
A WORLD ALMANAC EDUCATION GROUP COMPANY

Starfish was tired of living at the bottom of the sea, especially since Jellyfish had told her about other stars, half her size, that shined at night and got to dance around the sky.

"I don't shine down here," said Starfish, "and I'm tired of seeing only sand, fish, and coral. I want to dance around the sky! How can I get to the sky?" she asked Jellyfish and her minnow friend, Minnie.

"Ask the seahorses," they replied. "Maybe they can help you."

"We can take you as far as the ocean's surface," the seahorses offered.

"Then, let's go!" laughed Starfish. "Goodbye, everybody," she called happily to her friends. "Remember to look up and see me shine at night. I'll be the brightest star in the sky."

Jellyfish and Minnie were sad to see Starfish leave. They wondered if they would ever see their friend again.

"Here we are!" said the seahorses, arriving at the ocean's surface. "Now you'll have to . . ."

But before they could tell Starfish what to do next, a wave swept them up and sent them all flying in different directions.

"Whoa, there, little friend," chuckled Dolphin, catching Starfish on the tip of his nose. "I hear that you want to get to the sky. Of course! That's where stars shine. The sky is a long way up, but I'm very good at tossing. I'll get you there."

Dolphin leaped high into the air, again and again — and
again! But he just couldn't toss Starfish high enough.
"This job calls for a whale," Dolphin muttered.

"Here I am," sang a huge blue whale. "I can get Starfish to the sky! But we'll have to hurry, before those dark clouds move in."

Whale sent an enormous burst of water through her spout, shooting Starfish into the air. Starfish flew toward the sky, rising higher . . .

　　　　and higher . . .

. . . but not quickly enough. The dark clouds got there first.
Thunder was rumbling, and lightning was flashing. Starfish
couldn't see stars shining anywhere, and she was scared!

Just then, a tiny light broke through the clouds.
"Keep climbing," it said, "and don't be afraid."
So Starfish kept climbing until she was above the clouds . . .

. . . and saw thousands and thousands of stars.

"How spectacular!" cried Starfish. "Dolphin was right. The sky is where stars shine, and I belong here, alongside all the others."

"I see you're not scared anymore," said a voice nearby. It was Altair, one of the brightest stars in the sky. "But why don't you shine?" Altair asked.

Starfish told Altair that she had come from the sea and hadn't yet learned how to shine, but that she would like, very much, to dance around the sky with Altair, anyway.

"But I can't dance around the sky," Altair told Starfish. "I belong to the constellation Aquila, the Eagle. If I dance off somewhere, I will upset Aquila."

Starfish was disappointed that Altair couldn't dance with her, but she saw plenty of other stars she could ask.

Starfish asked big Denebola in the constellation Leo, and she asked all the twinkling stars in the constellations Cancer, Gemini, Taurus, and Aries. They couldn't dance with her, either!

Starfish became very sad. And when she got to the
constellation Pisces, the Fish, she started to miss her sea
friends terribly.

Seeing Starfish so sad, two tiny stars in Pisces broke the rules. They went to comfort her, but they just didn't understand. They didn't know anything about the bottom of the sea. They didn't know about Minnie, who could blow bubbles, or Jellyfish, who could hug you with his arms, or Dolphin, who could toss you into the air with the tip of his nose. When the stars in the sky looked down at Earth on a cloudless night, all they saw were the lights on in houses. Nothing more.

Suddenly, with a whoosh like a strong sea wind, a shooting star approached the unhappy starfish.

"I make wishes come true, little starfish," said the shooting star, "and I know your wish is to go back to the sea. Of course! That's where a starfish should be. Come with me."

The shooting star's wide, sparkling tail was incredibly powerful.
The moment Starfish hopped on, the two plunged toward Earth
at top speed.

"There's the sea," said the shooting star, a short while later. Starfish barely had time to say goodbye to her friend from the sky, when . . .

PLOP!

Down on the seafloor, the news spread quickly. Starfish had returned! Minnie, Jellyfish, Dolphin, and many other sea creatures rushed to greet her.

"You came back!" they all exclaimed.

"Thank goodness," thought Minnie.

"I was homesick," said Starfish. "The stars in the sky are all the same, and they have to stay in their places. They can't dance around at all!"

"Thank goodness," thought Jellyfish.

All the sea creatures gathered around as Starfish told them about the scary thunder and lightning, about Altair and Denebola and all of the other stars in the constellations, and about the shooting star with the sparkling tail.

"But shining isn't everything," Starfish said. "The bottom of the sea is where I'd rather be. It's much more colorful and interesting than the sky."

Jellyfish wrapped his arms around Starfish and gave her a big hug.

"Welcome home!" bubbled Minnie.

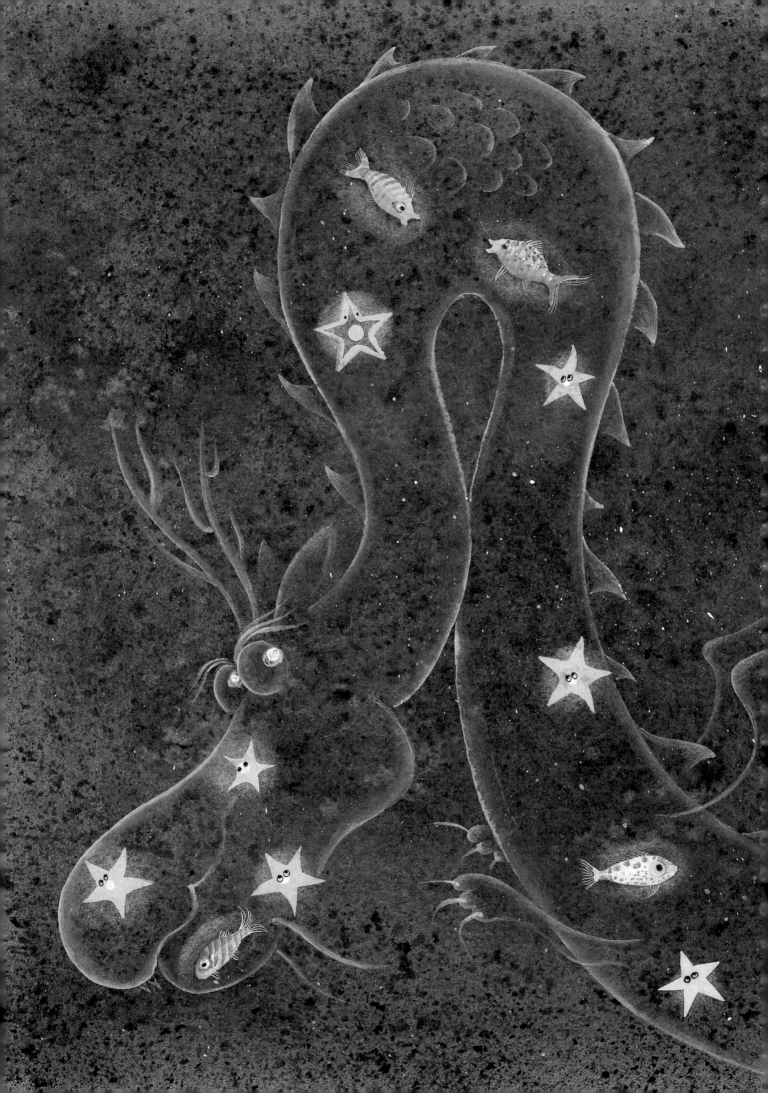